ADVENTURE ON KLICKITAT ISLAND

Hilary Horder Hippely

illustrated by Barbara Upton

PUFFIN BOOKS

For my son, Luke,
and for our friend and teacher,
Susan Ann Holmberg
H.H.H.

For my parents, Howard and Jean
B.U.

PUFFIN BOOKS
Published by the Penguin Group
Penguin Putnam Books for Young Readers, 345 Hudson Street, New York, New York 10014, U.S.A.
Penguin Books Ltd, 27 Wrights Lane, London W8 5TZ, England
Penguin Books Australia Ltd, Ringwood, Victoria, Australia
Penguin Books Canada Ltd, 10 Alcorn Avenue, Toronto, Ontario, Canada M4V 3B2
Penguin Books (N.Z.) Ltd, 182-190 Wairau Road, Auckland 10, New Zealand
Penguin Books Ltd, Registered Offices: Harmondsworth, Middlesex, England

First published in the United States of America by Dutton Children's Books, a member of Penguin Putnam Inc., 1998
Published by Puffin Books, a division of Penguin Putnam Books for Young Readers, 2000

10 9 8 7 6 5 4 3 2

THE LIBRARY OF CONGRESS HAS CATALOGED THE DUTTON EDITION AS FOLLOWS:
Hippely, Hillary Horder. Adventure on Klickitat Island/by Hillary Horder Hippely; illustrated by Barbara Upton. p. cm.
Summary: One dark, stormy autumn night a child hears the animals on Klickitat Island crying because they have no
shelter, and the child's Beary proposes a daring plan to help them. [1. Storms—Fiction. 2. Animals—Fiction. 3. Toys—
Fiction. 4. Stories in rhyme.] I. Upton, Barbara, ill. II. Title.
PZ8.3.H5565Ad 1998 [E]—dc21 97-38861 CIP AC

Puffin Books ISBN 0-14-056633-3

Printed in Hong Kong

One dark autumn evening,
the full moon was hiding;
I heard the wind moaning
and saw the sea rising.

"It's a storm," I told Beary
        and tucked him in tight.
"That noisy old thunder
        might rumble all night.

"But with Blankie around us
        there's nothing to fear;
at least we're not out
        with the eagles and deer.

"On Klickitat Island
        just think of the rains,
now soaking the otters
        and poor baby cranes."

Then I hummed for a while
    and was closing my eyes,
when I saw Beary jump up
    and to my surprise

he reached for his jacket—
    "Someone's calling," he said.
"We can't be much help
    if we stay here in bed!"

So I snatched up our blankie
    and quick as could be
we crept down the back stairs
    and ran to the sea.

Our dinghy was waiting
   by the creaky old dock;
we climbed in together
   and rowed past the rock.

Then waves pitched us so high
   and crashed us so low,
we almost lost track of
   which way we should go.

Up ahead loomed the island.
    "Row hard," I told Bear.
"We'll make it together—
    three pulls and we're there."

We took a deep breath
    when we stepped on the sand,
clutching our blankie
    and each other's hand.

The beach seemed deserted—
    it was so hard to see.
But who had been calling
    to Beary and me?

We heard a few sniffles,
   then somebody sneezed,
and a rabbit hopped out
   from under the trees.

He waved one big paw,
   so we ran to his side.
Such a pitiful sight!
   We both almost cried.

For there in a clearing
   huddled deer, birds, and otters—
so sad and bedraggled
   and drenched with storm waters!

"We're scared," explained Rabbit,
   "to be out in this storm.
We should all stay together—
   cozy and warm.

"But our nests and our burrows
   and our caves are too small.
We can't find a home
   the right size for us all."

Then together they cried,
   they wept for so long,
that I finally yelled, "Stop it!
   So much crying is wrong.

"We've brought you our blankie—
   we'll share it with you;
it helps us feel brave
   and will help you all, too.

"But first we need shelter
   from this dark, stormy sky.
We need to build something
   to keep us all dry."

"Build?" replied Eagle.
      "I'm an excellent scout.
I'll find the best sticks
      and twigs lying about."

"I'll fetch them," cried Moose.
      "Let me help," added Deer.
"I'll also haul driftwood—
      the beach is so near."

"How about clamshells?" said Otter.
　　"And seaweed and kelp?"
"How about brambles?" asked Rabbit.
　　"And boulders should help."

Two bears rolled the boulders
　　and piled them up high. . . .
They built a great fireplace
　　that reached toward the sky.

Then we propped and we piled
　　all the driftwood we'd found,
and plugged up the holes
　　from the roof to the ground.

"Rumble! Boom!" crashed the thunder,
　　but now no one cared;
with so much to work on,
　　how could we be scared?

With deer hauling driftwood
and cranes helping sort,
soon standing up tall
was a Klickitat fort!

For a moment we stood
   in that terrible weather,
amazed by the home
   we had all built together.

Then Moose led a cheer—
   "Hip hooray!" we all cried,
and hurried to fill up
   the warm space inside.

"Now a story," said Rabbit.
　　"It's time for a tale."
But right in the middle,
　　we heard a sad wail.

There sat an otter—
　　just a baby, so sweet.
"No one's sharing," he whimpered,
　　"I can't cover my feet!"

We pulled and we stretched
    to give him some blankie,
but it didn't quite reach
    so Bear gave him his hanky.

"Now I'm cozy," sighed Otter.
"I just wish I could eat!"
So his grandma concocted
the tastiest treat.

It was partly a cake
and partly a soup;
we all helped ourselves
from a long-handled scoop.

Before long we got sleepy
  by that warm fireside,
while the wind moaned and howled
  and the rain poured outside.

Soon an eagle was yawning
  by a young chickadee;
then the whole clan was snoring
  except Beary and me.

"Sleep tight," I told Beary,
  as I gave him a hug.
"We'll stay here till morning,
  safe, warm, and snug."

But the storm must have broken
   as we both lay there dreaming.
When we opened our eyes,
   the full moon was gleaming.

We tiptoed away
   so our friends wouldn't wake,
and we rowed the dark sea—
   now as still as a lake.

We woke in the morning,
   our room full of light,
but we know where to go
   the next dark, stormy night!